Mad Matt

JENNA KAY

Storyshares

Published by Storyshares, LLC.

The characters and events in this book are fictitious.
Any similarity to real persons, living or dead,
is entirely coincidental.

Storyshares
Storyshares, LLC
24 N. Bryn Mawr Avenue #340
Bryn Mawr, PA 19010-3304

www.storyshares.org

Aligned with the Science of Reading.

Interest Level: Ages 12+

ISBN 9798885974691

Book design by Storyshares

Storyshares

 **Storyshares**

GETTING STARTED

 These passages provide practice reading engaging and accessible connected text while supporting foundational literacy skills!

PRE-READING

- Review **phonics rules** that will help you decode the passage.
- **Preview** the text for examples of words that follow the rule(s).
- **Explore challenge words**. These are words the don't fit the decoding pattern.

WHILE READING

- **Read** as much as you can.
- Scoop the text into **meaningful phrases**.

AFTER READING

- **Summarize** the story.
- **Discuss** how you felt after reading. Was this a successful reading experience? Why or why not?
- Make a **prediction** for what will happen next.

SCOPE AND SEQUENCE

At Storyshares, we teach all six syllable types, in order of frequency in the English language, beginning with closed syllables, which account for just under 50 percent of English. This approach empowers students to read more, faster.

These passages are cumulatively decodable, meaning that the passages include words that help students practice phonics concepts that were taught earlier in the scope and sequence.

Consonant -le

R-Controlled Vowels

Vowel Teams

Vowel- Consonant-e

Schwa & Exceptions

Open Syllables

2+ Closed Syllables

Closed Syllables

⭐ **Skills covered in this set**

"Mad Matt"

/ a / sound

short "a"

add(ed)	cat	flash(ed)	lap	Nash	sad	tapped
at	chat	gasped	mad	Nat	sag	that
Babs	clapped	glad	mat	pal	sash	
back	class	grabbed	math	pass	sat	
bad	cracked	had	Matt	pat(ted)	slack	
black	dad	hat	Max	rap	snap(ped)	
brat	dashed	Jack	nap	rat	stat(s)	

challenge words

aw	looked	Mr.	ugh
hair	maybe	pssst	whispered
laughed	missed	smile	
liked	mom	thinking	

high-frequency regular words

across	did	let	this
after	got	like	up
be	head	not	will
but	in	on	with
can	it	room	yes

high-frequency irregular words

again	do	what
come	don't	

Matt was not mad.

Matt was sad.

"Pat Matt on the back," Matt's mom said to Matt's dad.

"Or he is sad," she added.

"I do pat Matt on the back, Babs," Matt's dad snapped. "I will," he added.

Matt sat in his room.

Matt's cat Max sat on the mat.

Matt patted his lap.

Max dashed up in a flash for a nap.

Max let his head sag on Matt's lap.

***

In Stats class, Matt tapped Jack's back.

"Pssst. Pass this to Nat?"

Nat looked back at Matt.

"Nat, can you chat after class?"

Nat's hair was black.

She had a sash across her back with a black cat on it.

"And that is that!" said Mr. Nash.

"Aw, snap," Matt gasped.

He was thinking of Nat and her black cat.

So he missed "that."

Again.

"Matt?"

It was Mr. Nash.

"The stat?"

Matt looked back. He grabbed at his hat.

He did not like math.

He had a flash of what Mom and Dad would say.

"Don't be a brat," Matt's dad would say.

"Matt is not a brat!" his mom would say.

"But don't slack, Matt," she would add. "And don't snap back."

***

"Matt?"

Ugh. Mr. Nash.

"Come back, Matt." He clapped.

Jack laughed.

Jack is a rat.

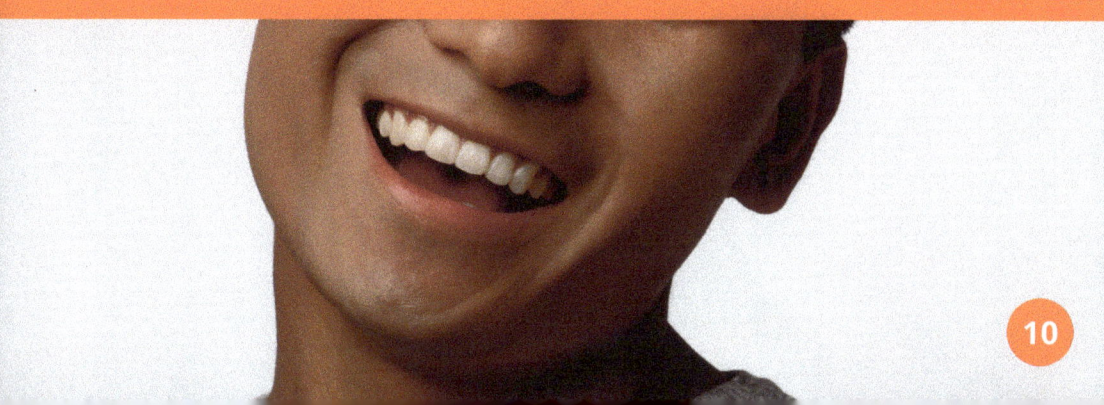

Matt was mad.

Nat looked back. With her black hair and her sash with a black cat.

Nat flashed a smile. "Don't snap," she whispered.

"Nat?" said Mr. Nash. "Got Matt's back?"

Matt cracked a smile.

Nat had his back.

Nat liked math. Nat liked Matt. Nat did not like Jack.

"Yes," said Nat.

Matt was glad.

Nat was glad.

Maybe it was not so bad.

Matt was not mad.

Matt had Nat.

Nat was his pal.

About the Author

Jenna Kay is a fiction writer who brings warmth and curiosity to every story she creates. Known for her keen eye for character and sharp sense of voice, she transforms everyday moments into narratives that resonate with readers of all ages. When she isn't writing, Jenna enjoys exploring local coffee shops, tending to her ever-growing collection of houseplants, and discovering new trails to hike.

About The Publisher

Storyshares is focused on supporting the millions of teens and adults who struggle with reading by creating a new shelf in the library specifically for them. The ever-growing collection features content that is compelling and culturally relevant for teens and adults, yet still readable at a range of lower reading levels.

Storyshares generates content by engaging deeply with writers, bringing together a community to create this new kind of book. With more intriguing and approachable stories to choose from, the teens and adults who have fallen behind are improving their skills and beginning to discover the joy of reading. For more information, visit storyshares.org.

Easy to Read. Hard to Put Down.

Scan to learn more and browse our collections

Thank you for using Storyshares, your Pathway to Literacy for striving readers in grades 3+.

Please keep in touch. We have...

- **Free Resources**
- **Intervention Curriculum for grades 6-12**
- **Decodable Chapter Book series for upper elementary, middle school, and high school**
- **A digital library with 500+ high-low and decodable titles**
- **Professional development for educators**

Follow Us

@storyshares

/StorysharesLiteracy

@storyshares

/company/story-shares

Continue the conversation!

www.storyshares.org

info@storyshares.org